MW00900141

# The Super Sandwich

Lynn George

# NEIGHBORHOOD READERS

Rosen Classroom Books & Materials™

New York

The people on Maple Street had a party.
Everyone who lives on Maple Street was there.
Everyone had a good time.

There were balloons everywhere.
The children played ball.
A band played music.

Everyone brought food to the party.
"Here are green peas," said Mrs. Bell.
"Here is a salad," said Mr. Smith.

Mr. Jones said, "Here is some corn."
Mrs. Chin said, "Here is a cake."
"Here is ice cream!" said Mr. Allen.

"We are going to make a huge sandwich," said Tina.
"It will be big enough for everyone to eat!"

"Here is the bread," said Sarah.
"Mrs. Lee baked this bread just for us."
"That is a lot of bread!" said Tom.
"We are going to make a huge sandwich!"
said Sarah.

**7**

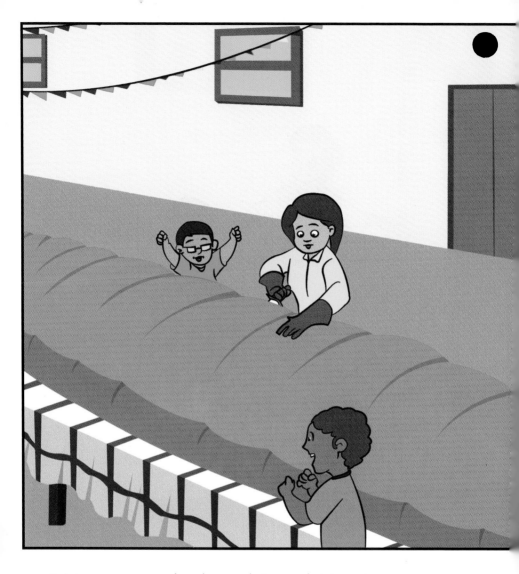

"We must cut the bread," said Mrs. Lee.
She cut and cut and cut.
At last the bread was ready.

Tom said, "Now we put on turkey."
They put on big pieces of turkey.
They put on small pieces of turkey.

"Let's put on cheese," said Sarah.
They put on yellow cheese.
They put on orange cheese.
They put on cheese with holes in it.

"Let's put on apples," Tina said.
They put on red apples.
They put on green apples.
They put on yellow apples.

Carlos said, "Let's put on tomatoes."
They put on green tomatoes.
They put on red tomatoes.
They put on yellow tomatoes.

Mike said, "Let's put on pickles."
They put on big pickles.
They put on small pickles.
They put on lots of pickles.

"Let's put on lettuce," said Tom.
They put on green lettuce.
They put on red lettuce.
They put on lots and lots of lettuce.

"Let's put on the top piece of bread," said Sarah.
Everyone helped.
"Our sandwich is ready," said Tina.
Tom said, "That's the biggest sandwich I've ever seen!"

**15**

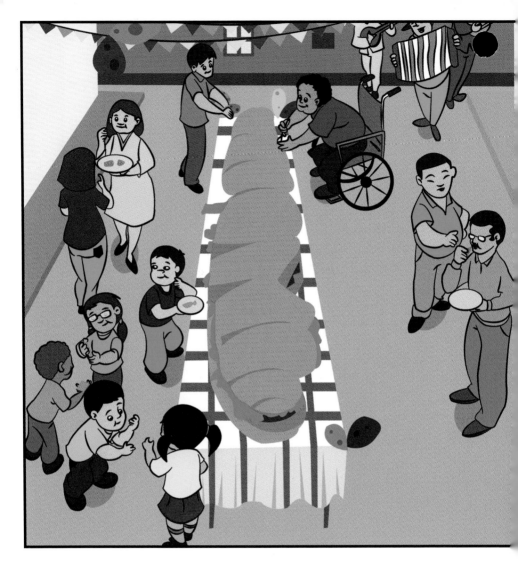

"Now we can eat our big sandwich!" said Tina.
"Come and eat!" called Carlos.
Everyone ate and ate.
The sandwich tasted super!